# Davy Crockett

Tale retold by Larry Dane Brimner
Illustrated by Donna Berger

Adviser: Dr. Alexa Sandmann, Professor of Literacy,
The University of Toledo; Member, International Reading Association

**COMPASS POINT BOOKS**

Minneapolis, Minnesota

Compass Point Books
3109 West 50th Street, #115
Minneapolis, MN 55410

Visit Compass Point Books on the Internet at *www.compasspointbooks.com*
or e-mail your request to *custserv@compasspointbooks.com*

**Dedication**
For Robert San Souci, who told me I could.
    -LDB

Photographs ©: Dave Bartruff/Corbis, 30.

Editor: Catherine Neitge
Designer: Les Tranby

**Library of Congress Cataloging-in-Publication Data**
The cataloging-in-publication data is on file with the Library of Congress.
ISBN 0-7565-0603-4
                    2003019950

# Table of Contents

## What a Guy!

He could run faster, dive deeper, stay under water longer—and come out drier than anyone this side of the big swamp. He was part-horse and part-alligator, with a touch of earthquake thrown in just for the rumble. He was Tennessee's own Davy Crockett.

"I'm a screamer," he bragged, meaning he was rough and tough and loud. "My father can outwrestle any man, and I can outwrestle my father. Why, I'm the best darn shot east OR west of the Big Muddy." That's what Davy called the mighty Mississippi River. "And if what I say

4

isn't true," he said, "then I wish to be kicked silly by a cricket."

Davy liked to boast about the things he could do, but sometimes that got him in trouble. Big trouble. There was the time he claimed he could grin raccoons right out of the trees. Nobody believed him. Davy sure didn't want to have the reputation of being a liar. No, sir. Everyone knows a reputation was everything to men of the frontier. So Davy decided to settle the matter once and for all.

Davy set off with the group of doubters to a spot way out back of the backwoods where, at last, he spied a raccoon. The critter was resting comfortably on a high branch in a tree.

"I'll double him up like a spare shirt," Davy said to the crowd. That was frontier talk that meant he planned to get it laughing so hard it would bend over and fall right out of the tree. Davy started grinning. He grinned for what seemed like forever. He grinned until his grin muscles were sore.

Not once did that varmint double up or even come close to it. It just kept grinning right back at Davy.

The whole episode set off Davy's temper. There was nothing to do but get his ax, cut down the tree, and teach that critter a lesson.

When the tree landed on the ground, Davy suddenly felt foolish. That darn raccoon was really a knot-hole glinting under the full moon.

Then Davy saw something else. "Look there!" he said. The bark around the knothole was gone. Davy had grinned it completely off! Davy had spoken the truth. He really could outgrin anything.

The fact is, Davy's tales were all true—all true, unless they were false.

## Davy Makes His Entrance

Not surprisingly, Davy Crockett started life in a most unusual way—although, for somebody destined to be an American legend it wasn't all that uncommon. Storks had nothing to do with it. No, by golly, Davy knew how to make an entrance. He rode into this world saddled to a streak of lightning. He landed near the Nolichucky River at a cabin owned by Mr. and Mrs. Crockett, who wept with joy to see such a big, strong, beautiful baby.

How big? The fact is, Davy was the biggest infant that ever was. He was so big his feet stuck out the end of an absolutely HUGE cradle that was made out of the shell of an absolutely HUGE snapping turtle.

He was also smart—the smartest child that ever will be. Why, he was smart enough to talk to the critters that roamed his neighborhood and understand them when they talked back. Of course, such an infant meant that Mr. and Mrs. Crockett had to make a few changes. One of them was to replace the family's chickens with rattlesnakes because Davy wouldn't stop crying until he'd had at least one omelet made from 12 fresh rattlesnake eggs.

Davy kept right on growing bigger and stronger. When neighbors wanted to build a bridge across the river, they called on Davy. One whack with his ax was all it took to lay down a tree, and that wasn't even using the cutting side. His arm worked like a piston in a steam engine, and tree after tree fell.

Then Davy, like any good neighbor, helped sink those timbers into the water. One good jump on top of a timber would sink it just right. He had to be careful, though. Two jumps would make a timber disappear beneath the muddy river bottom.

## Sally Saves the Day

Boys grow into men, and so it was with Davy—if you can imagine him growing to a size bigger than he already was.

One morning at the crack of dawn, Davy had a thought. "I think it's time to find me a wife," he said.

Mrs. Crockett fixed Davy a good breakfast. He had 10 bear steaks, 20 flapjacks, 30 rattlesnake eggs (scrambled), and 40 pans of grits (baked). He washed it all down with 50 jugs of vinegar. Then he whistled for his dogs, Tiger, Grizzle, and Rough—the ugliest strays

anywhere—and off they went through the Tennessee timber.

By and by, Davy got sleepy. Looking for a wife was hard work, after all. He decided there'd be no harm in a nap. So he rested his head in the fork of a tree and before long, his snores were blowing up a gale.

Davy slept until something pulled at his hair. Suddenly, he was awake, but just the same, he kept his eyes closed. He planned a surprise attack of his own to teach a lesson to the good-for-nothing so-and-so that was disturbing his sleep.

When he felt another tug, Davy yelled with such fury that every last leaf dropped from the tree and the sky turned yellow. He threatened to make pudding out of his tormentor, but when he tried to get up, he discovered he was in a pickle. His head was stuck!

Davy bellowed. He moaned. He even tried to bargain with the

varmint. "A fair fight is all I ask, sir," Davy said. "I'll give you $5 if you help me out of this situation. Then I'll whip you into pudding." The tugging didn't stop.

He endured more than a dead possum could stand. Then, while he still had most of his hair left, he heard something crashing through the trees like a roaring river. The dogs took off like a shot and Davy thought, *I'm a goner.*

As fate would have it, though, Davy wasn't a goner at all.

"I'm Sally Ann Thunder Ann Whirlwind," a voice said. "Looks to me like you're in a pinch. Those eagles are tearing out your hair and using it to build themselves a mighty fine nest."

"Pleased to meet you, ma'am," said Davy, remembering his manners. "Do you think you could drive them away?"

"Can I drive them away?" she guffawed. "Why, they're no match for me! Just you watch."

Then Sally pulled a young tree out of the ground and knocked down two of the critters. With a rip-roaring yell, she screamed the feathers off the other four and ended up with the first-ever *really* bald eagles. The poor creatures were so embarrassed that they hightailed it to other parts.

19

"You're a pretty sad sight," Sally said to Davy. Then she grabbed some baby rattlesnakes that just happened to be passing by. She hooked them together to make a good, strong rope, and pulled Davy free.

After Davy's head slipped loose, he got a good look at Sally Ann Thunder Ann Whirlwind for the very first time. She was a strapping girl, with arms as big as tree trunks. "Whoa! You're a regular steamboat," said Davy, smitten. "I knew I'd find myself a wife if only I used my head."

That's just what he had done.

20

## Capturing a Comet

Now that Davy had a wife, he needed to think of some way to earn a living. Being an American legend was fun, but it didn't pay the bills. He thought he'd try farming. The problem with farming, he soon learned, was that it was hard work and it didn't allow a person time to nap. Oh, that Davy Crockett was fond of his naps!

Then Davy had another idea. "I'll go into politics," he said, because everyone knows that politicians don't overwork themselves. Most days they nap from sunrise till moonset. So Davy set out on foot to meet his neighbors near and far, all across that great wilderness. He told every single one of them about all the things he could do, and, by golly, they voted for him, each and every one. That's how Davy Crockett got to Congress and had one of his greatest adventures ever.

It all began when the president of the United States stopped by Congress one day, looking every bit as anxious as a hound dog cornered by a pack of angry porcupines. "We're doomed," the president told Congress. "My scientific advisers tell me a giant comet is speeding head-long toward the Capitol. Unless somebody has a notion about how to stop the fiery beast, it's going to blow us and the whole world into tiny bits. And that's a fact."

As you might expect, there wasn't a single idea worthy of consideration in the whole of Congress. It all made

Davy tired, and he stood up to stretch his legs. "Of course!" said the president, taking notice of Davy. "Why didn't I think of it before? Mr. Crockett, you'd be doing us all a mighty favor if you'd capture that comet and send it elsewhere."

Capturing a comet sounded a heap more entertaining to Davy than listening to the president and other members of Congress fret about it, so he agreed to do what he could. He whistled up his pet bear, Death-Hug, and set off lickety-split to the top of the Allegheny Mountains.

From the top of the highest peak, Davy saw the comet. It was monstrous big—the biggest thing Davy had ever seen—but it wasn't headed for the Capitol. It was aiming straight at Davy!

Davy readied himself, and when the ball of spittin' fire got within reach, he thrust one arm out and snatched it right out of the sky. He twisted and twisted until he completely wrung off its tail. Then he pitched both parts back into space beyond the farthest stars.

Davy returned to Congress after the adventure, sporting blistered hands. The comet had even scorched some of his hair right off! (Luckily, Sally Ann Thunder Ann Whirlwind Crockett had recently caught a raccoon, so Davy began wearing the critter to keep his head warm.) In a quiet ceremony, the president declared that Davy Crockett was a hero for saving the world. Publicly, he declared himself a hero for thinking of Davy in the first place. Presidents can be like that.

The comet? The comet was so confused that to this day it is wandering around space trying to figure out just where it is in the universe. And it is still trying to find its tail.

# The Real Davy Crockett

1786    The real Davy was born near Limestone, Tennessee, on August 17.

1806    Married Polly Finley.

1815    Wife Polly died.

1816    Married Elizabeth Patton, a widow whose husband had left her well off.

1821    Elected to the Tennessee state legislature.

1827    Elected to the United States Congress; reelected in 1829 and 1833.

1835    The first Crockett *Almanack* is published.

1836    Killed at the Alamo in San Antonio, Texas, on March 6.

Washington, D.C. ★

• Limestone

Texas

• The Alamo

---

Davy Crockett (1786–1836) was a real man who became a legend even during his own lifetime. He was known for his entertaining public speeches that exaggerated truth and invented events—tall tales, if you will. Many of Crockett's tales were written in two books: *Sketches and Eccentricities of Col. David Crockett, of West Tennessee* (1833) and *A Narrative of the Life of David Crockett* (1834). Both books brought Davy widespread fame.

In 1835, Davy Crockett's *Almanack* was published. A series of other almanacs followed. They were all small paperbound books, similar to comic books today, that included stories about Davy's frontier adventures, as well as other tales. They were instantly successful, and their popularity only soared after Davy's death while fighting at the Alamo in the Texas Revolution. New editions continued to be published until 1856.

28

# Tennessee Grits

You can't be from Tennessee—or anywhere else in the South—and not like grits. Serve them anytime you like, but it's a fixture at breakfast. Here's a recipe a frontiersman like Davy would love! It makes four servings.

1 cup grits, regular or quick-cooking
1/2 pound sharp cheddar cheese, grated
8 tablespoons butter

3 eggs, beaten
1/3 cup milk

Preheat the oven to 350°.
Prepare grits according to package directions. Stir in the cheese, butter, eggs, and milk. Pour the mixture into a buttered 3-cup baking dish. Bake 40 minutes, or until set. Serve hot with butter. Some people add a drizzle of syrup to top things off.

29

# Glossary

**exaggerated**—enlarged, made bigger

**gale**—a strong wind

**guffawed**—a burst of loud laughter

**piston**—part of an engine that moves up and down within a tube

**reputation**—what others think of a person

**smitten**—in love

**tormentor**—a person or thing that causes pain to others

**varmint**—an annoying person or animal

*A statue of Davy Crockett stands in the town square of Lawrenceburg, Tennessee.*

# Did You Know?

➤ Davy Crockett's first scrape with school didn't go well. He got into a fight on his fourth day there, and, fearing that either the teacher or his father would whip him, he ran away. He didn't learn to read and write until after he turned 16.

➤ The Alamo was a small fortress in San Antonio commanded by Colonel William Travis. Davy Crockett was one of 150 men fighting to help free Texas from Mexico. They were badly outnumbered. More than 5,000 Mexican soldiers surrounded the Alamo. "Liberty and independence forever!" Davy wrote in his journal before he was killed.

➤ Davy Crockett was a legend when he died. He became a bigger legend with the help of Walt Disney, who first televised the series "Davy Crockett Indian Fighter" on December 15, 1954.

# Want to Know More?

## At the Library

Adler, David A. *A Picture Book of Davy Crockett.* New York: Holiday House, 1996.

Osborne, Mary Pope. *American Tall Tales.* New York: Alfred A. Knopf, 1991.

Schanzer, Rosalyn. *Davy Crockett Saves the World.* New York: HarperCollins Publishers, 2001.

Walker, Paul Robert. *Big Men, Big Country.* San Diego: Harcourt Brace Jovanovich, 1993.

## On the Web

For more information on **Davy Crockett,** use FactHound to track down Web sites related to this book.

1. Go to *www.compasspointbooks.com/ facthound*
2. Type in this book ID: 0756506034
3. Click on the *Fetch It* button.

Your trusty FactHound will fetch the best Web sites for you!

## Through the Mail

**Texas Historical Commission**
P.O. Box 12776
Austin, TX 78711
To get information about the Alamo

## On the Road

**Davy Crockett Birthplace State Park**
245 Davy Crockett Park Road
Limestone, TN 37681-5825
*www.state.tn.us/environment/ parks/davyshp*
To visit a museum at Davy Crockett's birthplace

**David Crockett State Park**
1400 W. Gaines
Lawrenceburg, TN 38464
931/762-9408
To visit the site along Shoal Creek where Davy Crockett had a powder-mill, gristmill, and distillery

# Index

**About the Author**

Larry Dane Brimner has written more than 100 books for children, including the award-winning *Merry Christmas, Old Armadillo* (Boyds Mills Press) and *The Littlest Wolf* (HarperCollins Publishers). He is also the reteller of several other Tall Tales, including *Calamity Jane, Captain Stormalong, Casey Jones,* and *Molly Pitcher.* Mr. Brimner lives in Tucson, Arizona, in the shade of the giant saguaros.

**About the Illustrator**

Donna Berger is a freelance illustrator and marketing consultant based in Chelmsford, Massachusetts. She studied art at the Cleveland Museum of Art and at the Cleveland Institute of Art. She attended Bowling Green State University in Ohio and received a Bachelor of Arts degree from Cameron University in Oklahoma.